For Dana, the other half of Team Messy Book
– M. P. T.

For Henry, Darcey, and Gertruda
– R. S.

tiger tales
5 River Road, Suite 128, Wilton, CT 06897
Published in the United States 2016
Originally published in Great Britain 2016 by Little Tiger Press
Concept by Dana Brown and Maudie Powell-Tuck
Text by Maudie Powell-Tuck
Text copyright © 2016 Little Tiger Press
Illustrations copyright © 2016 Richard Smythe
ISBN-13: 978-1-68010-037-2
ISBN-10: 1-68010-037-8
Printed in China
LTP/1800/1435/0216

For more insight and activities, visit us at www.tigertalesbooks.com

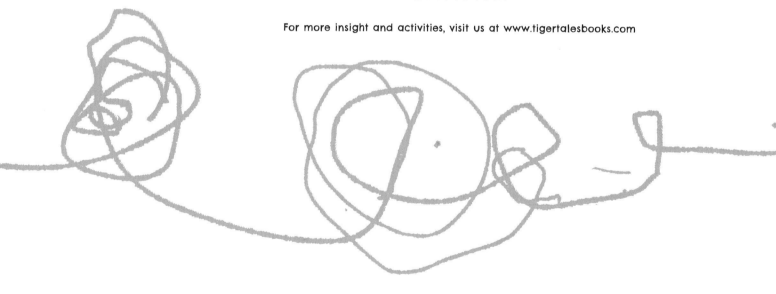

The MESSY BOOK

by Maudie Powell-Tuck • Illustrated by Richard Smythe

tiger tales

But cleaning is *boring.*

We could hide the mess under my bed . . .

or blow it up . . .

. . . or eat it.

That is NOT the right way
to clean.

RUMBLE
RUMBLE
RUMBLE

Woo hoo! Everything is back where it belongs. No more mess!